For Erik, Maya, Lola, and Kai, who are always up for a group hug.

And for my mom, who first taught me to blow kisses. — B.S.

For Kim and Rosie, with love. — S.H.

CLEVER
• Publishing •

Text copyright © 2021 by **Bianca Schulze**
Illustrations copyright © 2021 by **Samara Hardy**

First published in the United States of America in January 2021 by "Clever-Media-Group" LLC
www.clever-publishing.com
CLEVER is a registered trademark of "Clever-Media-Group" LLC

ISBN 978-1-951100-43-8 (hardcover)

For information about permission to reproduce selections from this book, write to:
CLEVER PUBLISHING
79 MADISON AVENUE; 8TH FLOOR
NEW YORK, NY 10016

For general inquiries, contact: info@clever-publishing.com

To place an order for Clever Publishing books, please contact The Quarto Group:
sales@quarto.com • Tel: (+1) 800-328-0590

Art created with Procreate and Adobe Photoshop
Book design by Michelle Martinez

MANUFACTURED, PRINTED, AND ASSEMBLED IN CHINA
10 9 8 7 6 5 4 3 2

WHO LoveS the DRAGON?

by
BIANCA SCHULZE

illustrated by
SAMARA HARDY

A little closer.

A little more.

Whoa!
Too close . . .

. . . **especially** for how Dragon's feeling right now.

5

An unhappy dragon can be a bit **fierce** and **fiery**—
literally.

How about we count to **ten** together and give her time to cool off?

Start here

1 2 3 4 5

6 7 8 9 10!

You see, today is the annual **FRIENDSHIP FESTIVAL!**
Dragon has been looking forward to the festivities all year long.

It's one of the
happiest, most heartwarming,
most happening events of the year.

It's a day to be spent with loved ones wandering through markets, listening to merry musicians,

visiting the fortune-teller, watching jesters juggle, knights joust,

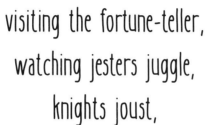

and—most importantly—feasting together.

Alas, all of Dragon's
friends are just
too busy.

Where are they all going?

Oh no!

Wave goodbye to the cooks.

ENCHANTED FOREST

CASTLE

PALACE

DEEP WATER

12

They were called away to cater a delicious dinner for the king and queen.

Meanwhile, the noisy knights were last seen (and heard) riding away into the Enchanted Forest.

YIPPEE!

WOO-HOO!

14

Look at them! They're so fun and silly.
It's no wonder Dragon enjoys spending time with them.

WHEE!

YAHOO!

Blow a kiss
as they go!

15

Dragon's heart is feeling as heavy as a stone.

We need your help to cheer her up.
We need to show Dragon some love.

Nod your head and blink twice
if you think you can help?

Thank you!

Let's share some kind, powerful words.
Hey, Dragon — you know who's **wonderful**?
You are! Even when you're having a bad day.

Joyous SMART awesome

~Kind~ SUPERB

lovely UNIQUE amazing

Beautiful

Your turn. Put your hand on your heart and tell Dragon something kind.

Beautifully said!

There's definitely less smoke flaring from her nostrils.

Now, let's give her scales a nice, long stroke.

Do you know what makes me feel good on a bad day?
Laughing. Let's try telling her a joke.

Why are dragons such good storytellers?
· · · · · · · · · · · · · · · · · · · ·
Because they all have funny *tails*!

Ooh!

Was that a little snort
of laughter we heard?

Something else that cheers me up is listening to my favorite song and dancing.

Perhaps it's *time* to move around!

We can giggle, jiggle, and wiggle our way to feeling happier.
Show Dragon your favorite dance moves, and then
maybe she'll show us hers.

Wiggle

Jiggle

Giggle

**Wait a second.
Freeze!**

Something isn't right . . .

Yikes!
What happened?

We were doing so well.

Don't worry. How about we try marching with our feet?

Don't stop!

Keep marching!

Wow! Nice save! You and Dragon are looking good.

High fives all around!

After all that moving and grooving, let's take a moment
for some deep belly breaths. Dragon-style, of course.

Lie down flat. Relax your scales.

Breathe in through your nose and out through your mouth.

(Be extra careful not
to breathe out any fire!)

Oops!

I think we've done it.
We've helped Dragon feel better!

Wait a second . . .

do you hear that?

There's a lot of commotion coming from outside.
It sounds like Dragon's name is being chanted.

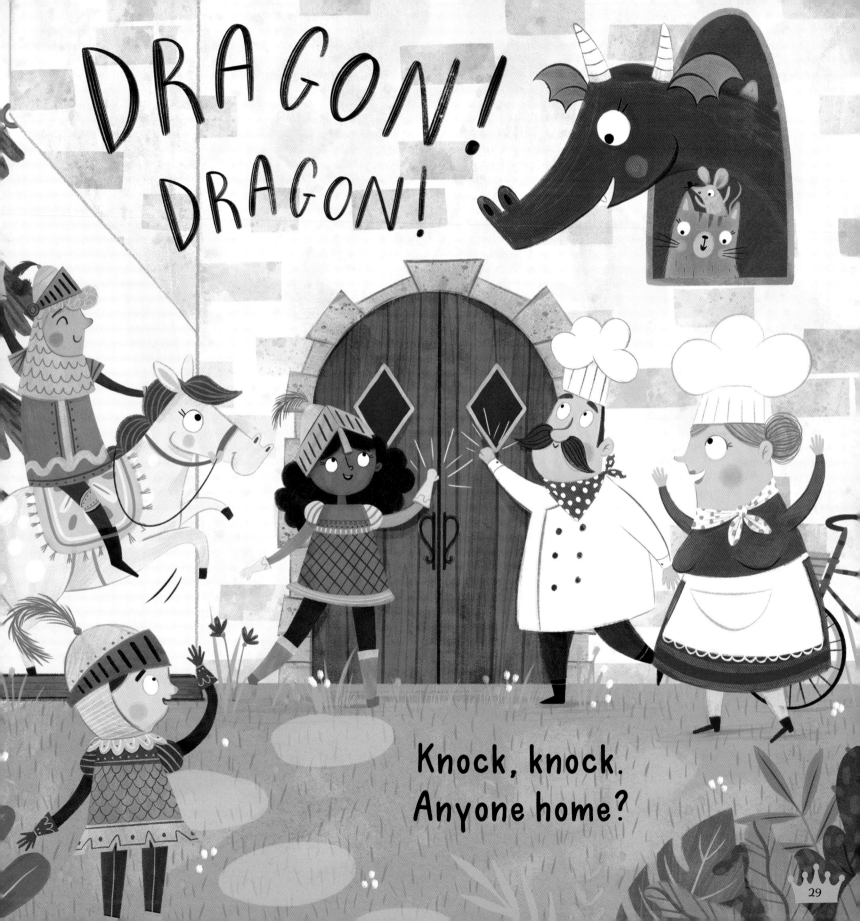

DRAGON! DRAGON!

Knock, knock.
Anyone home?

29

SURPRISE, DRAGON!

30

We'll always make time for the ones we love.
And we love you so much, Dragon!

A celebration like this needs some confetti!
Shake the book, and we'll see what happens.

Hooray! I think a group hug is in order, **don't you?**

WE ♥ DRAGON!

After you close the book, hold and squeeze it tight.
Dragon wants **you** to feel loved, too!